8 Class Pets
+1 Squirrel
÷1 Dog=
CHAOS

8 Class Pets
+1 Squirrel
÷1 Dog=
CHAOS

by **Vivian Vande Velde**

illustrated by
Steve Björkman

Holiday House / New York

HOLIDAY HOUSE is registered in the U.S. Patent and Trademark Office.
Printed and Bound in October 2011 at Maple Vail, York, PA, USA.
www.holidayhouse.com
First Edition
1   3   5   7   9   10   8   6   4   2

Library of Congress Cataloging-in-Publication Data

Vande Velde, Vivian.
8 class pets + one squirrel [divided by] one dog = chaos / by Vivian Vande Velde ;
illustrated by Steve Björkman. — 1st ed.
p. cm.
Title uses division sign.
Summary: A dog chases a squirrel into an elementary school one night, creating
monumental chaos.
ISBN 978-0-8234-2364-4 (hardcover)
[1. Schools—Fiction.   2. Animals—Fiction.   3. Humorous stories.]
I. Björkman, Steve, ill.   II. Title.   III. Title: Eight class pets plus one squirrel
divided by one dog equals chaos.
PZ7.V377Aag 2012
[Fic]—dc22
2010048153

To those teachers
who are bold enough
to have a class pet
in their rooms

Contents

8 Class Pets
+1 Squirrel
÷1 Dog=
CHAOS

TWITCH
(school-yard squirrel)

Being a squirrel is the best thing in the world.

The next best thing in the world is living where I live—which is near School. School is where humans send their young to learn things.

I don't know why.

Squirrel mothers teach their own young. These are things my squirrel mother taught me:

★ how to climb
★ how to land when I jump or fall

- ★ how to find food
- ★ how to bury food
- ★ how to find food after I've buried it
- ★ how to look cute enough that humans will give me food, so I don't have to find it, bury it, or find it again
- ★ how to get along with animals that don't eat squirrels (Not eating squirrels is something I admire in those I meet.)
- ★ how to get away from animals that DO eat squirrels

These are all valuable lessons for a squirrel.

I'm not sure why humans can't teach their own young.

A few of the children are all right at climbing, but most aren't good at finding food, and they're hopeless at burying food.

A squirrel mother teaches her young all they need to know by the end of summer, but human children spend *five years* in School. Five years is long enough for a squirrel to grow very, very old, so it's a good thing we're faster learners.

And the humans aren't even truly finished in five years!

I have heard them talking, and I know. Before they go

to School, they go to Kindergarten. And after they leave School, they will go to someplace that is called Middle School. And after *that*, they will go to High School.

I haven't seen any of these other places. I have no idea what Kindergarten is. But by their names, I'm guessing Middle School is halfway up, and High School must be at the very top of a tall tree. I suppose that's the only way the humans will ever teach some of those young ones to climb.

But School and the yards around it are a good place to live.

It's fun to climb up the School building and to play on the playground equipment when the children aren't using it. There are also trees for climbing, and some of them are nut trees and some of them are fruit trees. That's two of my big interests rolled into one: climbing and eating.

And the people who live here love squirrels.

They're always buying toys and exercise equipment for us, and they set these things up around a feeder to make sure we notice them—it's a mini-playground with a snack bar in the middle. Some of the toys are for twirling on, and there are ropes to shinny up and climb down, and balance beams to walk across. Sometimes, to make things extra-challenging for our benefit, the ropes and poles are greased to make them slippery. Whee!

It's very considerate of people to give us these jungle gyms so we don't become fat and lazy, like, for example, the groundhog.

One day I was exploring a new bird feeder in the yard next door to School. It had a big slippery disk for sliding on, and I was having so much fun, I lost track of the time.

Then I realized that the air had turned cool, and shadows were growing long. Evening is a dangerous time of day because certain creatures who are not squirrels and who are not fat and lazy groundhogs start thinking about dinner. Or breakfast. Some of them start thinking of a meal that involves squirrel.

I looked up. And there was an owl, and she was flying straight at me—as though *I* was the main course on the snack bar!

All I could do was start running in a zigzag pattern to try to confuse that owl.

I didn't even notice the dog who was napping in his front yard.

Now, it's easy to point a finger—or paw—in blame, but I say; if that dog didn't want me running over his nose, he shouldn't have had it resting on the ground between his paws. But, anyway, the next thing I knew, the dog was chasing me, too. He ran so hard, he broke the leash that was supposed to hold him in his yard.

Luckily, one of the humans who works at School had left the door propped open.

I noticed the big banner:

WELCOME!

This is the same banner that tells the children School is open again after the summer.

Someone was obviously telling me School was open for me to escape from the dog.

Didn't I say the people here love squirrels?

So for the first time in my life, I ran into School.

That owl veered away and flew off into the evening.

But the dog followed me in.

GREEN EGGS AND HAMSTER
(first-grade hamster)

I am a hamster, and I live in Mrs. Duran's first-grade classroom. Mrs. Duran named me after a famous book. She says that makes me a literary pet. *Literary* is the biggest word I know, but I don't know what it means.

Mrs. Duran reads a lot of books to the first-graders. The boys and girls talk about what happened in the story and tell if they liked it. Sometimes they write their own stories. I don't have a pencil to write stories, so I run around in my exercise wheel instead. Round,

round, round I go. Sometimes I get so dizzy, I forget things.

Did I mention I'm a hamster?

The children also do art projects. They color, they cut with scissors, they paste. Lately, they've been very excited about some project they're doing out in the hall. I have a project, too, but it's inside my cage. Mrs. Duran gives me tissue and cardboard, and I rip them up with my teeth to make a nice and soft and cozy bed. Every morning Mrs. Duran cleans out the bed I made the day before, along with my litter, and I get to start all over again on a brand-new art project.

Maybe that's what *literary* means.

My favorite part of first grade—after snack time—is that the children and I have been learning about numbers and how to count. There are all sorts of things I can count:

1. I have 4 legs and 1 tail. ($4 + 1 = 5$, even though my tail is shorter than my legs.)
2. There are 2 levels in my cage. Level 1 is the top level, which has my bed and my food bowl and a mirror for me to look into. Level 2 is the bottom level, which has my water bottle and my wheel. I also have a chew toy in the shape of

an elephant. (2 levels + 1 bed + 1 food bowl + 1 mirror + 1 water bottle + 1 wheel + 1 elephant to chew on = lots of things for Green Eggs and Hamster to do.)

3. The ladder from downstairs to upstairs has 10 rungs. The ladder from upstairs to downstairs also has 10 rungs. This is because it is the same ladder. (1 ladder = 1 ladder.)
4. The number of Special Hamster Treats I can fit into my cheek pouches at one time is 8. (8 special treats = yummy.)

There is a squirrel named Twitch who lives outside. Twitch sometimes comes and sits on the window ledge to visit. Twitch is good at cramming birdseed into his cheeks, but he says birdseeds are too small to count. *I* think that Twitch is not very good at counting.

I am too good a friend to tell him so.

One day, after the children had gone home, after Mrs. Duran had gone home, after the custodian had swept the floor and turned off the lights but before it got dark, I was busy counting the numbers on the wall clock. There are usually twelve numbers—unless I count them after I've gone around in my exercise wheel. Then there are a lot more numbers. *And* they move.

This day I had counted seventeen numbers when Twitch came running into the room.

Did I say Twitch is a squirrel?

"Help, help!" Twitch called. "There's a dog chasing me."

I didn't ask why a dog was chasing him. Sometimes details are important, but sometimes they're not. I got an idea, so I said, "Climb up on the bookshelves behind me. And hide behind the dictionary." The dictionary is the biggest book in the room.

Twitch was up there before I could say, "Wow! You're a good climber!"

And then the dog ran into the room. Attached to his collar was a long length of rope, which dragged along behind him. "Where's that no-good squirrel?" the dog barked at me.

I scratched my ear and asked, "Did you check the room with the snake?" (There are five grades in this school, and Mrs. Shaughnessey's fifth grade, where the snake lives = the farthest room from Mrs. Duran's room.)

The dog growled, "I smell that squirrel here."

"Are you sure you don't smell me?" I asked. "The squirrel and I are both rodents, and that makes us cousins. 1 squirrel + 1 hamster = 2 rodent cousins."

The dog sniffed at my cage. "Maybe," he said.

"Where's the room with the snake?"

"Fifth grade," I said. "All the way down the hall."

The dog left, his rope leash still trailing him. But just when Twitch started to come out from behind the dictionary, the custodian came in. Twitch ducked down again.

"I thought I heard a dog," the custodian said.

"He's gone to the fifth grade," I said.

But even though animals can understand people, most people aren't very good at understanding animals.

The custodian looked around, scratched his head, and said, "Must be outside the building. Good. A dog in the school is the last thing I need with that art contest tomorrow."

As soon as the custodian was gone, Twitch climbed back down the bookshelves. "Thanks, cousin," he said. "See you tomorrow."

He ran out of Mrs. Duran's room but was back before I could climb into my exercise wheel.

"Oh no!" he said. "The human has left School— and he shut the door behind him. That dog and I are both locked in here. What should I do?"

This was too much for me. I had thought of 1 plan, but I couldn't think of 2. "Go next door and ask the rabbit," I said. "She likes to order everyone around, but she's smart. She'll think of something."

MISS LUCY COTTONTAIL
(second-grade rabbit)

It's not everybody that starts school in second grade.

The children in Ms. Walters's class went to first grade last year. They were in a different building in kindergarten the year before that. And most of them spent a year or two in nursery school.

Not me. I came to second grade straight from the pet shop, so that shows I'm the smartest one here. Well maybe, except for Ms. Walters.

But I'm not sure.

Ms. Walters never talks about being in first grade,

so I think she may have skipped first grade, too. But she does talk about last year's second-grade class. I'm smart enough to know that means Ms. Walters was kept back. But I am polite enough not to mention it.

I plan to finish second grade in one year. In fact, I think I may well skip third grade and go directly to fourth.

Another way I know I'm the smartest one here is that Ms. Walters tells the children their job is to learn, but she says that my job is to be cute and cuddly and not bite. Obviously, I have already learned everything there is to learn.

Sometimes the children forget to latch my cage. I help them learn by running around the classroom and hiding under things. I leave a trail of little poops to help them find me.

Once, I made it all the way across the hall to Mr. Daly's third-grade room. Mr. Daly has fish. The fish are in a tank, and the tank is on a cart with wheels. I don't think the fish are very smart at all. They *never* escape and hide under things. They just swim back and forth, back and forth. I held my long, good-at-hearing-everything ears up against the glass to listen. But all they'd say was "We are in a school. We are in a school."

"I know," I said. "We all are."

There's a squirrel who lives outside. Sometimes he comes to visit after Ms. Walters and all the children have gone home. The squirrel sits on the windowsill and makes faces and says rude things like: "If you were really smart, the humans couldn't catch you. I don't let them catch me."

I point out to him that *I* don't have to stay outside when it's cold or rainy and that *I* don't have to find my own food.

The squirrel says squirrels are smarter than rabbits. He says the kids in the playground sometimes call one another "dumb bunny." Nobody, he says, ever calls another person "dumb squirrel."

I think the squirrel is making this up. I've never

heard anybody say "dumb bunny." One time, though, I heard one of the third-graders call me "Mr. Fuzz-butt" instead of "Miss Lucy Cottontail."

This is one of the reasons I'd like to skip third grade. But I don't tell the squirrel that.

Besides, this just shows how dumb that third-grader was: He couldn't even read the sign over my cage. I'm surprised Ms. Walters ever let him out of second grade.

One day, after the children had spent most of the afternoon learning something that had to do with crayons and glitter sticks, I was taking an afternoon nap when I heard a dog barking. He sounded so close, it was as if he was in the building. But that couldn't be. Dogs don't go to regular school. They have their own school to go to because they aren't smart like rabbits and children.

But the next thing I knew, in ran that squirrel. If dogs aren't smart enough to go to school with the rest of us, squirrels *definitely* aren't smart enough. They'd be kept back for… like… three years in a row and have to sit in the corner the whole time.

"Help!" the squirrel said.

"Go away," I said.

"There's a dog chasing me," the squirrel said.

I told him, "Then you shouldn't have done whatever it was you did to make him chase you."

"I didn't do it on purpose," the squirrel said.

I chewed at an itchy spot on my foot. "If you were as smart as you think, these things wouldn't happen."

The squirrel said, "I told Green Eggs and Hamster you were too stuck up to help me."

I may be smart, but I am not stuck up.

While I was still busy chewing, the dog ran by my room, never looking into the doorway. The end of the long rope that was attached to his collar bumped and went *thwap* against the walls. Across the hall I could hear the dog barking at the hamster, "There was no squirrel there with the snake. You're hiding him."

The squirrel was still standing there in front of my cage, shaking, too dumb to move.

Apparently, I had to tell him everything. "Run now," I said. "While the dog is in the first grade. Go back out the way you came in."

"The door is closed now." The squirrel's teeth were chattering from fright. "Please hide me."

I felt sorry for him. "Go to the room next to where the hamster is. There's a rat there."

The rat has sometimes come to visit my second-grade classroom. He's very good with his little hands, and he can open his own cage and doesn't need to wait for a child to forget to latch it. This doesn't make him smarter than me—he's just clever with his hands.

"Sweetie," the squirrel said.

Cheeky thing! "I beg your pardon," I snapped frostily.

"The rat's name is Sweetie."

"I knew that," I said. "Ask Sweetie to let you in. The dog won't be able to get at you if you're in a cage." I couldn't resist adding, "Because inside a cage is safer than outside."

"Yeah, yeah," the squirrel said, waving his tail at me as he turned and ran.

SWEETIE
(library rat)

I like being a rat, even though rats sometimes have a bad reputation.

For example, if a person tattles or does something mean, another person might say: "You rat!"

I never tattle, and I'm not mean.

Sometimes when the parents of the students first meet me, they ask Miss Krause: "Does he bite?"

Miss Krause answers: "Does your dog bite? Would you keep him if he did? No, Sweetie doesn't bite."

Then she'll hand me a treat to show them. I stand

up on my back feet and wiggle my pink nose. (I have heard people say this is cute, and I'm working hard to impress them.) Then I take the treat very gently from Miss Krause and I eat it, holding it with my fingers.

Another thing people say, if something is dirty and worn, is that the thing is ratty. I am not dirty or worn looking. I have white fur, and I spend a good deal of time grooming it. (Since the fur is mine and since I am a rat, the fur is ratty—but it is also clean and neat.)

And if someone has messy hair, people call it a rat's nest. There you have me: I *am* a bit messy because I love to chew on things. (Not fingers—but just about everything else.)

Every year, the first story Miss Krause reads to the incoming first-graders is *Cinderella*. Some of the children complain that they already know the story, but Miss Krause says she wants to start the year with a story that has a good rat role model. The rat in *Cinderella* is the hero of the story because he drives the coach that carries Cinderella to the ball. Without the rat coachman, Cinderella wouldn't even meet the prince.

I love to hear stories—even when the hero is someone else besides a rat.

My friend Twitch the squirrel often comes after school to visit me. (He's too shy to sit on the window ledge when the children are there because they move too fast when they see him.) Twitch calls me "cousin" and tells me stories about Outside. I tell him stories made up from bits and pieces of the ones I've heard from Miss Krause and the children.

In my stories the hero is often a rat.

In Twitch's stories the bad guy is always an owl.

One day Twitch came, not to the window ledge, but running into the library.

"Help!" he said.

I started to say, "What's—" But before I could finish asking, a dog ran in.

Rats can't see very well, which is why, when we are loose in a room, we like to stay near the walls. But we are excellent at sniffing. I could smell the dog right away. He smelled angry. And then I heard him.

"There you are!" the dog barked at Twitch. "You'll make a tasty supper!"

In stories, that would be called showing a character's intentions.

I guess owls aren't the only ones who can be bad guys in a squirrel's story.

Twitch ran up the leg of the table where my cage sits. He grabbed hold of the bars of my cage and said, "Cousin! Help!"

"Back off!" I yelled at the dog, trying to make my voice big and fierce.

The dog was not impressed. His barks were a lot scarier than my squeaks. He jumped at us. He wasn't tall enough to be able to jump onto the table where Twitch and I were, but he almost made it. He jumped again, and got a little higher—so that the nails of his front paws scratched the wood of the table as he tried to hold on but couldn't.

Twitch said to me, "The rabbit says you can open your cage and let me in."

"Good idea!" (That rabbit is *very* smart.)

I jiggled the latch.

The dog jumped again. His front part landed on the table, but the weight of his back end made him slide off again. For a moment he got tangled up in his own long, long leash. But only for a moment. He took a few steps away to get a running start.

"Twitch!" I said. "Let go of the door. I can't swing it open with you holding on."

Twitch let go, I swung the door open, and Twitch ran in. I slammed the door shut.

Safe!

The dog leaped, and this time he landed on the table.

But he was going so fast, he slid and rammed right into the cage, knocking us into the display of art books Miss Krause had set up.

21

Books and cage and Twitch and I went flying off the back edge of the table.

I was dizzier than the time Miss Krause put me in an exercise ball and one of the boys kicked it across the reading area. Except nobody was calling for a time-out for this dog.

The cage had landed on its side, and I could see that the door had not only popped open, it was bent back. It would not close. The cage was no longer someplace to be safe from the dog.

The dog was looking a bit confused to find the cage wasn't on the table anymore, but then he spotted us on the floor, and he jumped down.

"Run!" I yelled to Twitch.

A SCHOOL OF NEON TETRAS
(third-grade fish)

We are in a school.

We are in a school in a school.

We are tickled by that idea.

The people who come to look at us call us neon tetras. We don't know about that—we just know that we are.

Each of us has bright blue stripes and bright red stripes. We shine in the dark. We are very beautiful. Even one of us would be very beautiful. But we aren't one. We are a school.

We live in the water. Of course. We don't understand how other creatures live out of the water and breathe the air. But some of them do.

Our water is surrounded by glass that gives it a square shape. Living in the water with us are some plants and a catfish who eats the slime off the sides of the glass. She does not have blue stripes, she does not have red stripes, she is not beautiful, and she doesn't have much to say. But she keeps our water clean.

Sharing the water with us, but not living, is a shipwreck and a miniature man with a treasure chest that opens and closes. In the treasure chest are sparkly gems. On the floor of our square pond are sparkly stones. Neither the gems nor the stones are as sparkly as we are.

We dart back and forth in our glass-enclosed pond and around the shipwreck.

We are a school.

Outside of the glass that forms the boundary of our

pond is a man who feeds us fish flakes and frozen brine shrimp. (Yum! Frozen brine shrimp!)

There are also little men out there who press their faces against our glass. Our man who feeds us calls these little men "boys and girls." He says to them, "Boys and girls, do not tap on the glass. Do not lean on the cart and make it move." Sometimes they do anyway, when he's not looking.

When they do, we dart back and forth.

Our favorite part of the day is global studies. The globe the little men study is a big round thing that shows the world. Most of the world is water.

That idea tickles us.

So, beyond our pond there is the room with the man and the little men and the globe; beyond that, there is more glass, which is called "windows." Beyond that glass is the world, and now we have seen on the globe that most of this is water.

One of the air-breathers who sometimes looks in through the windows is a creature that calls himself squirrel.

One day the squirrel came swimming through the air into our room. He came with another creature, a small white creature with a long pink tail. But they were not in a school, because they were not the same.

They did not look the same, and they did not move the same.

The squirrel said, "Help! The dog is going to eat us."

We said, "There is protection in a school."

The second creature, the one who was not a squirrel, put his ear up to the glass that protects us from the air. We said again, so that he could hear, "There is protection in a school."

The nonsquirrel repeated this for the squirrel.

The squirrel said, "What?"

We said, "When you swim in a school, only some get eaten, while the rest stay safe. You need to find a school."

When his friend told him this, the squirrel said, "Neither one of us wants to get eaten."

A creature bigger than either of them entered the room.

Bigger often eat smaller.

This big creature said, "Stop running, you sorry waste of fur!"

The squirrel darted in one direction, and the squirrel's friend darted in another.

"In a school!" we told them.

The big noisy creature followed the squirrel, knocking into one of the desks where, during the day, one of the little men sits. The desk tipped over, and books and papers and pencils fell out.

The big noisy creature continued to follow the squirrel. The big noisy creature had something trailing from him, the way sometimes a crab will have seaweed trailing from itself. It was long and white, and it got wrapped around things, and it knocked over a big plant by the man's desk. Dirt and leaves fell out.

The big noisy creature tried to follow the squirrel up onto the man's desk, and that sent more books and papers and pencils onto the floor. A picture of the man's family fell as well, and his souvenir mug from MarineLand—which looks like a wondrous place.

The squirrel went up the stand that holds the globe. But then he stepped onto the globe. The globe spun. The squirrel spun. The squirrel flew through the air and landed on the big noisy creature's head.

The big noisy creature was so startled, he made his own water right there on the floor.

The squirrel and his friend darted out the door.

"In a school!" we called after them.

The big noisy creature followed them.

But the long white thing that was not seaweed must have gotten wrapped around the cart that makes our pond move, the cart that the little men are not supposed to lean on.

We began to move, dragged along by the big noisy creature. Our pond swayed and bumped behind him as he ran.

We continued to swim, safe, in a school, in a school.

LENORE
(fourth-grade parrot)

Hola!

That's one of my favorite words because I come from Puerto Rico, and that's how people there say "hello." The Spanish for "please" is *por favor*, and "thank you" is *gracias*. Those three words cover a variety of situations.

Another of my favorite words is "Nevermore" because that's a refrain in a poem called "The Raven." A refrain is a word you say over and over. I like to say words over and over.

But I don't like to say, "Polly wants a cracker." I don't know why some people think I should.

My name isn't even Polly. My name is Lenore, and it comes from that same raven poem.

But I'm not a raven. I am a blue and gold macaw, which is a kind of parrot.

Luckily, I *love* poetry. My owner—her name is Rosa DaSilva—she says that since we both come from Puerto Rico, poetry is in our blood. (Along with our accents, I guess.) Here is a poem I have been working on:

Sitting in the trees,
I sometimes sneeze
as loud as you please.
With a beak as big as mine,
you need to draw the line,
or a sneeze will rattle your knees.

Okay, okay, I'm still working on it.

Some of those fourth-graders, believe me, their poems aren't any better.

Good poetry or bad, I like being in school with Rosa and the kids.

When Rosa first got me, she'd leave me home while she went to the school to teach. All day long, nobody else was there: Mr. DaSilva works in a bank;

the DaSilva kids go to their own schools. Being alone made me crazy. I started to pluck my feathers. That made *Rosa* crazy. She was like, "Eeek! I'm going to end up with a bald bird!"

Now she brings me to the classroom where she teaches. The kids there call her Mrs. DaSilva instead of Rosa. When we're in school, I have to remember to call her Mrs. DaSilva, too.

Such a chore, such a bore:
Not Rosa, *por favor.*
It's Mrs. DaSilva in school.
That is the rule
if I wanna be cool.

This is hard to remember. I also have to remember there are other words I'm not supposed to say in school, either.

I think school has too many rules.

Sometimes if Rosa and her family have to go someplace and stay out late, she'll leave me here in the classroom overnight. That's okay; I don't mind. Once in a while.

That's how I got to meet the squirrel.

This is what happened: One day this squirrel, he comes running in—I've seen him before, but I don't know his name—and he's got this big ugly dog chasing him.

And the dog's got a fish tank on a rolling cart chasing *him*.

The squirrel, he can't fly, but he knows *up* is safer than *down*. He goes running up the stand that holds my cage, then he sits on top and yells down to the dog, "You're ugly, and your mother has fleas."

I don't know about the mama with the fleas, but I think to myself, Surely this dog can't argue about ugly.

Señor Dog, he's jumping up in the air, trying to tip the cage over, and he goes, "Yeah, you rodent? You come down here and say that."

The water in the fish tank is going *slosh! slosh!*

"Whoa, *chicos!*" I tell them. "Careful of the innocent bystander!"

There's a little rat, too, but *Señor* Dog isn't interested in him—just the squirrel. The rat calls up to the squirrel, "I'll get help so there's more of us, like the fish said."

The dog keeps barking, so I start squawking. The squirrel is making my cage sway like the boat that brought me here. I say to the squirrel, "You ever hear the term *seasick?*"

Next thing I know, the rat comes running back in with a hamster and a rabbit.

It's like a convention of small mammals.

Plus fish.

But the dog, he ignores them all and keeps yapping at the squirrel.

And those small mammal guys, they don't know what to do. They're just running around in circles. The rat squeaks, "Somebody do something!" The hamster is trying to count how many of them there are, but every time somebody moves, he loses track and has to start all over. The rabbit is full of useless advice. She's all like: "Don't let him get you!"

I think the squirrel already thought of that.

The fish look like they're beginning to get seasick, too.

Then Wham! Bam! That clumsy dog knocks my cage down.

My feathers are ruffled, but I don't get hurt, because I land on a pile of papier-mâché fruits and vegetables the kids have been making for some sort of art contest.

"Sorry!" the squirrel says to me as he dashes for the door, but the dog, he's so rude, he never says a

word of apology. He's just all: "Get back here, you...
you... squirrel!"

The fish, still dragged along behind on that bump-
ing, swaying, sloshing cart, are all like, "*Glug, glug.*"

The rat and the others, they start to follow.
I squawk:

"*Hola!* Don't leave me here on the floor
as you go out the door,
without even a 'Nevermore.'"

The rat is the only one left, slowest because he's
always staying close to the walls, not wanting to cross
the open space of the room.

So he comes back and unlatches my cage.

NANCY
(art room turtle)

Sometimes people who come to visit Mrs. Hinkle's room get confused. They ask, "Is he a turtle or a tortoise?"

Mrs. Hinkle says, "*Nancy* is a *she*, not a he. And *she* is a turtle."

Mrs. Hinkle and I, we think there's a big difference between turtles and tortoises. We can't see how people get confused.

By the end of a year of art class, Mrs. Hinkle's students will never again be the kind of people who get confused about this.

Tortoises live on dry land, but we turtles spend most of our time in the water, but sometimes we like to have dry land to crawl up on. My beautiful glass case has both, along with a nice heat lamp to keep me warm. Mmmm. Nice and warm and cozy. Mmmmm...

I'm sorry. I fell asleep there under the lamp.

Where was I?

Oh yes, I am a mud turtle, so I'll never grow bigger than six inches. This makes me the right size for Mrs. Hinkle to sometimes take me out of my glass case and set me on the table so the boys and girls can see me better. "Don't poke at Nancy or try to pick her up," Mrs. Hinkle says. "She's very shy."

It's nice to have someone else around to explain that you're not unfriendly but only shy.

Mrs. Hinkle teaches art.

Even though I'm shy, I like that the children ask if I can come out of my case so they can use me as a model. Mrs. Hinkle gives me a piece of melon or lettuce to munch on so that I will stay still and not explore the table too much while my picture is being drawn.

I like to have my picture drawn.

But I also like to draw my own pictures.

Sometimes Mrs. Hinkle pours food coloring onto

a piece of foil and lets me walk through it. Then she sets down a piece of art paper and I walk onto that, leaving colored footprints with my little webbed feet.

"We don't put paint on a turtle's shell," Mrs. Hinkle says. "But a little bit of food coloring won't hurt Nancy's feet."

One afternoon, after waking up from a nap and finding that all the children—and Mrs. Hinkle, too—had left, I was admiring all the new pictures Mrs. Hinkle had hung up that day. The children had been very excited and had talked about the artist who would be visiting the next day—an artist who was going from school to school to judge pictures and give out prizes for the best pictures. I think the best pictures are the ones with me in them.

But all of a sudden there was a commotion in the hall, so I pulled myself into my shell in case there was danger.

Good thing, because the noise came into the classroom. A dog was barking, a parrot was squawking, a squirrel was shouting, "Help! Help! The nasty, smelly dog wants to eat me!" and a hamster, a rabbit, and a rat were yelling, "Run, Twitch, run!" The wheels of the cart the dog was pulling went *squeak! squeal!* And the fish in the tank on the cart were yelling in their tiny fish voices, "School! School!"

Even with my head tucked safely inside my shell, I could see well enough to tell that Twitch must be the squirrel, since the others were telling Twitch to run and it was the squirrel who ran up onto one of the tables where Mrs. Hinkle keeps her art supplies.

The dog jumped up there, too.

So much energy! It nearly wore me out to watch them!

Twitch leaped off the table and over to the bookshelves, pulling himself up by *Art in Western Civilization,* and the dog couldn't follow, because the rope that tied him to the leg of the cart wasn't long enough. The dog ran back and forth on the table, knocking over paints and brushes and a box of chalk. The paint was leaking and dripped off the edge of the table, making a puddle on the floor.

I liked the slow, thick way that paint dripped, dripped, dripped... Mmmmm...

Where was I?

Oh yes.

I recognized Twitch, since sometimes I'd seen him look into the window of the classroom. Still, because I'm shy, I'd never talked to him before. But now that he was in danger, I wanted to help. It's scary when someone wants to eat you. I called over, "Excuse me? Mr. Squirrel, sir?"

This was very abrupt of me. Turtle manners call for long and slow and proper introductions. But this was an emergency. I said, "Don't you have a hard shell you can escape into?"

"Nope," Twitch said, springing from one book case to another. "Just fur."

Fur is not nearly as useful as a hard shell. I asked, "Do you have a stink gland?"

"Don't I wish!" Twitch bounded from the bookcase to Mrs. Hinkle's desk, to her chair, to the floor.

My goodness! Could he move fast!

The dog could move fast, too. But when he jumped off the art table, his fish-tank cart swung around and knocked into my table.

My case tipped. I pulled all the way into my shell again.

My case teetered. I closed my eyes.

My case tottered. Over the edge and onto the floor my case went, landing on its side. I rolled right out of it.

By the time I decided I was still alive, Twitch had already escaped into the hall. The dog, still attached to the cart, ran out of the room, with the parrot flapping her wings at him, and the hamster, the rabbit, and the rat scurrying pretty fast, too.

The dog had left a trail of painted footprints from the table to the door. It was mean of him to want to eat Twitch. But—I do have to say—he was a very talented artist.

I decided to follow.

ANGEL
(fifth-grade corn snake)

Sassafras.

Isn't that an absolutely delicious sounding word?

I simply love saying "SSSassssafrassss."

Society also has succulent syllables. As does *suspicious.*

The society I'm in is Mrs. Shaughnessey's fifth-grade classroom.

Suspicious is how outsiders sometimes react to me because I'm a snake. They say I'm sneaky and slithery and have slimy skin.

Sneaky and slithery, yes. But stroke my skin and see: I'm not the slightest bit slimy.

I have no fangs, no venom; I'm a simple orange and black and red corn snake, as long as a fifth-grader is tall.

Mrs. Shaughnessey's syllabus is history. Sassafras! History is such an interesting subject—besides being an amusing thing for a snake to say! "Hisssstory."

After classes I'm somewhat solitary. A squirrel sometimes peeks in the window, but he slinks down again as soon as he spies me. Doesn't he know he's too substantial a mouthful for a snake my size to swallow?

Only once a week I sup—mostly on frozen mice supplied by Mrs. Shaughnessey. Six out of seven days I could be a safe associate to all the other class pets, including the albino rat who sometimes scurries past my doorway, fast, as though suspecting I would feast on him.

It must be nice to have sensitive fingers to unfasten one's cell as one wishes and explore the school's silent halls.

So I was pleased one after-school afternoon when a ruckus spilled down the hall and into Mrs. Shaughnessey's classroom.

My tongue tasted a shift in the atmosphere.

The squirrel and rat burst onto the scene, along with a hamster (another excellent word!) and a rabbit. From the hall came the sounds of a dog snarling,

"Leave me alone—this has nothing to do with you!" while a parrot squawked, "*Olé! Olé!* Keep away!"

In the classroom, the hamster saw me and squeaked, "Yikes! This is the fifth grade—where the snake lives! Snake = danger!"

The squirrel tried to skedaddle and shoved the rabbit, who stood betwixt him and the door. But the rabbit snapped, "The snake's locked up, but the dog isn't—you're safer in here."

So the squirrel hastened for higher ground instead. Up the window blinds he scurried, though they swayed beneath his weight and smacked against the glass. From there, it was a short distance to the long narrow tube above the blackboard, where the historic maps are scrolled. The squirrel paced back and forth above "Medieval Europe" and "Renaissance Cities."

From the hallway, we caught occasional glimpses of the dog as he sprinted from classroom to classroom, trying to escape the parrot's beak. For some reason I could not discern, the dog was towing a fish tank on a pushcart. And from a slight distance a sociable but slow-moving voice called down the hall, "Hey, guys? Don't move so fast."

In Mrs. Shaughnessey's classroom, the nervous hamster ran around in circles and said, "That turtle carries her shell around with her for protection. Protection against dogs. Protection against snakes. Could we make some sort of a shell for Twitch?"

The rabbit was looking at the shelves where Mrs. Shaughnessey keeps my supplies, including the large, lidless SNAKE TRANSPORT box. The rabbit suggested, "Or a shell to cover the dog?"

I deciphered the rabbit's scheme. I myself do not like dogs—who snip and snarl and sometimes eat a poor harmless snake who has no poison to protect himself. So I said, "I could help."

The squirrel had misstepped and was dangling from the cord that lowers the maps. "How?" he asked. "By eating me before the dog has a chance to?"

"I've had my frozen mouse this week," I said. "My stomach is satisfied till Tuesday."

They all said, "Yech."

"Set me free," I said. "I'll distract the dog while some of you push that SNAKE TRANSPORT box off the shelf. Timed just right, it should tip over on top of him and hold him safe from eating any of us. I would never be so discourteous as to snack on schoolmates. Except, perhaps, on Tuesdays. Besides, history teaches us that we are stronger with allies."

"Allies," the rat repeated. "Like fish in a school."

"Trussst," I encouraged them.

The rat—fearless, steadfast rat—scurried to my enclosure and shoved that screen aside.

Just then the dog ran in, still attached to his cart and snarling, "Where's that less-than-worthless squirrel?"

The squirrel tried to scamper back up the cord, unscrolling "Renaissance Cities" till Florence was on the floor.

The blue and gold macaw flew into the classroom and squawked:

"*Señor* Dog's on the loose,
so move your caboose.

Everyone to your places.
Pretend you're at the races."

No one told the bird her meter was off.

I slithered onto the floor. Seeing me, the dog scuttled in reverse. If he could have scaled up his fish cart, I suspect he would have. He didn't notice the squir-

rel, the rat, and the hamster climb onto the shelf and begin shoving at that SNAKE TRANSPORT carton. The macaw saw, and went to their support.

The box moved closer and closer to the edge of the shelf.

I hissed, posing as ferocious, causing the dog to back up closer and closer to the overhang of the shelf.

The rabbit thumped her back leg, and the vibration was the last assistance that suspended receptacle needed.

Over the edge SNAKE TRANSPORT tipped, showering pine shavings on all. But the fit and our timing were flawless. The box landed just so, to trap that dog—but not the cart—inside.

"Sassafras!" I said.

GALILEO AND NEWTON
(science lab geckos)

GALILEO: Most geckos sleep by day…

NEWTON: But we are day geckos.

GALILEO: So we sleep by night…

NEWTON: And are awake during the day.

GALILEO: Just like the students in Mr. Russell's science lab.

NEWTON: Well, most of them. Some of those students seem to like to sleep during the day.

GALILEO: Our scientific family name is Gekkonidae.

NEWTON: And our genus name is Phelsuma. We are—

GALILEO: Reptiles.

NEWTON: We live in a vivarium...

GALILEO: Where there are plants...

NEWTON: And bamboo to climb on...

GALILEO: And crickets and mealworms to eat.

NEWTON: Sometimes we get mangoes. I like mangoes.

GALILEO: I know you do. I prefer the houseflies, which are crunchier.

NEWTON: But not as sweet.

GALILEO: Mr. Russell teaches science.

NEWTON: We like science.

GALILEO: Every year Mr. Russell has a science fair.

NEWTON: We especially like the science fair.

GALILEO: It's fun and instructional.

NEWTON: That's what Mr. Russell says.

GALILEO: I was quoting him.

NEWTON: Quoting is fine, copying is wrong.

GALILEO: I know that.

NEWTON: The students make replicas of the solar system.

GALILEO: And the human eye.

NEWTON: And volcanoes.

GALILEO: I like the volcanoes.

NEWTON: They do experiments with helium...

GALILEO: And fruit flies.

NEWTON: Sometimes we get the leftover fruit flies.

GALILEO: Some of the children bring their pets in and do a report on them.

NEWTON: We've seen kittens.

GALILEO: And tree toads.

NEWTON: And mice.

GALILEO: And worms.

NEWTON: I don't think the worms were pets.

GALILEO: Sometimes they do a special report on us.

NEWTON: We are very photogenic.

GALILEO: We never blink when the camera's flash goes off.

NEWTON: That's because we don't have eyelids.

GALILEO: We've seen demonstrations on fire safety.

NEWTON: And the Heimlich maneuver.

GALILEO: And how to make paper.

NEWTON: Sometimes things go wrong.

GALILEO: Not often.

NEWTON: But sometimes.

GALILEO: Sometimes things go very wrong.

NEWTON: That's how we knew what to do when the squirrel, the hamster—

GALILEO: The rabbit, the rat—

NEWTON: The macaw—

GALILEO: And the snake! Don't forget the snake!

NEWTON: I wasn't going to forget the snake.

GALILEO: They came into our room.

NEWTON: They said the dog was going to get loose from the box and come after them.

GALILEO: They said it was an emergency.

NEWTON: We know what to do in case of an emergency: Dial—

GALILEO: Dial 911!

NEWTON: I was going to say that.

GALILEO: I said it already. You can say the next part.

NEWTON: But that was the exciting part.

GALILEO: The next part is exciting, too.

NEWTON: Not as.

GALILEO: Stop sulking.

NEWTON: Dial 911!

GALILEO: I already said that.

NEWTON: Now we've both said it.

GALILEO: Yes, Newton, now we've both said it. Only I said it first.

NEWTON: So they asked: "What does Dial 911 mean?"

GALILEO: And we showed them the telephone.

NEWTON: I showed them the telephone.

GALILEO: I showed it, too.

NEWTON: I showed it first.

GALILEO: Luckily, the hamster knows his numbers.

NEWTON: And the snake was able to knock the phone to where the rat could reach it.

GALILEO: The rat has dexterous fingers and pressed the buttons.

NEWTON: The macaw yelled, "Help! Help!"

GALILEO: The squirrel knocked some beakers on the floor, so there was the sound of breaking glass.

NEWTON: The rabbit screamed.

GALILEO: I never heard a rabbit scream before.

NEWTON: Somebody should mention it in a science fair report.

GALILEO: The emergency people came fast.

NEWTON: They always come fast.

GALILEO: By then the snake was falling asleep because he's a reptile—

NEWTON: Like us—

GALILEO: And he needed to go back to his vivarium with the heat lamp.

NEWTON: We like our heat lamp.

GALILEO: And the turtle likes hers. She kept saying, "Wait for me, guys." She didn't catch up till—

NEWTON: The principal came.

GALILEO: His face was almost as red and splotchy as the snake's belly.

NEWTON: That means he was mad.

GALILEO: I was *telling* that by *showing*.

NEWTON: It took a long time to round up all the animals.

GALILEO: Except for us, because we were still here.

NEWTON: And the fish were still in their tank, even though their tank was in the wrong room.

GALILEO: And the turtle wasn't hard to catch.

NEWTON: Neither was the snake, asleep on our floor.

GALILEO: The squirrel ran outside during the confusion.

NEWTON: So all that leaves is the dog.

GALILEO: Do you know the scientific name for dog?

NEWTON: Of course I do. It's—

GALILEO: Family Canidae, genus Canis.

NEWTON: You always like to get the last word in, Galileo.

GALILEO: No, I don't.

NEWTON: Yes, you do.

GALILEO: Do not.

NEWTON: Do.

GALILEO: Not always.

CUDDLES
(the principal's dog)

Master lives right next door to the school he owns, so I get to see him a lot. Sometimes he brings me to meet the children there. This would be a perfect place to live—except for that nasty squirrel Twitch.

Twitch acts like he owns the yard.

He eats the seeds Master puts out for the birds.

He jumps from tree to tree just out of reach and calls down to me that people like squirrels better than they like dogs. He says that's why Master ties me to a long rope leash when I'm in the yard. He says that's why Master puts me on a short chain leash when we go for a walk.

"No leash for me, nuh-uh," Twitch brags.

He runs back and forth just beyond where the leash stretches to. He says, "Ha-ha! Your master doesn't make me wear a collar and leash to keep me in one place. He must not trust you, Cuddles."

Twitch seems to wait for me to be watching before he'll climb into the garbage can at the edge of the playground. "Oh, Cuddles!" he'll say. "There's wonderful, tasty garbage in here today! Here's a French fry! And half a baloney sandwich! And some macaroni and cheese! I can't remember: Do you like macaroni and cheese, Cuddles?"

I stand there drooling, knowing I can't cross the short distance to get into that delightful-sounding garbage can.

Sometimes the only way to avoid Twitch is to go to sleep.

That's what I was doing when Twitch ran right over my nose.

Yow! That hurt!

I just knew he did it on purpose, and I went running after him. I was so mad that I ran so fast that the rope leash broke. I kept on running, pulling that long rope with me.

An owl was chasing Twitch, too. I don't know what Twitch did to get *her* mad. But I saw Twitch was heading for the school. The man who works for Master cleaning and repairing the building had hung a big banner over the door that said WELCOME because Master had invited special guests to come the next day. The man had left the door open while he was putting his ladder back in his truck.

"Don't you *dare* go into Master's school," I shouted at Twitch.

Guess what.

He ignored me.

In he went, as though he owned the place—just the way he acts as though he owns the yard.

The owl knew school was off-limits. "He's all yours," she said, winging away.

I was in the right. But the trouble was, all the pets took Twitch's side.

From room to room I went, chasing Twitch. A few things got knocked down or spilled or broken—but it was all Twitch's fault.

Those pets all worked together—even animals that *shouldn't* work together.

Finally, they knocked a big box on top of me. It was dark in there. I wasn't sure if that snake had been trapped inside with me or not, because the pine shavings kind of smelled like him. He didn't look like the kind of snake who bites, but you can't trust snakes. I hunkered down and sat quiet.

I could hear the pets laughing out in the hall and having a good time together. It was like a party!

The squirrel was telling jokes—mostly to do with me.

And the hamster and the parrot were telling everyone about how their names came from books, and they were all acting like that was a big deal.

And the rabbit was saying they needed to get out and get together more often—and they had to figure out a way for the squirrel to join them, too! And she asked the rat if he could open all the cages again the next day.

And the rat said yes, in between carrying on about something or other to do with Cinderella.

And the turtle said they could all work on an art project together.

And the geckos were saying they knew how to make a working volcano, and did anyone want to see?

Even the fish were saying something—I don't know what—it was too bubbly for me to understand.

I wasn't hearing the snake, which was part of the reason I suspected he was under the box with me. But I had just decided I needed to get out from under there—snake or no snake—when suddenly there were sirens, and people came rushing in, shouting, "This is the police."

I heard the pets scatter, then someone lifted the box off me.

No snake, but I saw something worse.

The person who had lifted the box was Master.

"Cuddles, Cuddles, what have you done?" he asked. "Bad dog. *Bad* dog."

I tried to tell him about the squirrel—and about what the pets were planning—but Master has trouble understanding more than the simplest things I say. He usually gets "I'm hungry," and "I want to play," and "I gotta poop or pee," but that's about it. He obviously had no idea what I was saying there in the school.

He had just taken hold of my collar when other people ran into the room. Some had black hats and shiny badges, and some had red helmets and boots and a hose.

"Is there a thief?" shouted one of the men.

"Is there a disorderly conduct?" shouted another of the men.

"Is there a fire in the walls?" shouted a third.

And the fourth asked, "Do you need us to knock a hole in the wall?" And he raised a sharp ax.

"No!" Master cried. "No! No! No!" He sounded upset. *Upset* means "danger."

Any dog knows that.

I lunged forward and barked at the man with the ax, barking, "Back! Back! Back!"

Master held on to my collar. "Cuddles!" he ordered. "Sit."

I sat because that's what a well-behaved dog does. But I kept on growling to warn the man that he'd better be on *his* best behavior, too.

The man with the ax backed up so quickly, he
knocked into the man with the hose. The man with
the hose backed up so quickly, he tripped over the box
that had covered me. He fell, and must have done
something to the hose because suddenly water shot
out of it. Whoosh! The water hit Master so hard, it
knocked him down on his bottom.

"Stop!" Master spluttered.

The man with the hose turned the stream of water
away from Master. *Whoosh!* It caught one of the
shiny-badges men, causing *him* to land on *his* bottom.

I bit at the stream of water to tell it that it was
bad. The man with the hose ran away still holding the
hose, so that it squirted at the desks instead of at the
people, but for some reason Master didn't thank me
for saving him.

Once they got the water turned off, Master locked me in his office while he and the men with the badges and the men with the helmets rounded up the pets.

It took a long time.

Master was still wet when he came to get me. He was also tired and grumpy.

He took hold of my collar and held onto it all the way out of the school, across the school yard, across the backyard, and into the house, with his shoes going squish! squish! squish!

"Cuddles," Master said, "I don't know what got into you. Tomorrow was supposed to be a special day."

I hung my head. I hung my tail.

Master crouched down beside me and looked deep into my eyes. He said, "I bet you have a story to tell." Then he said, "And I wish you could tell me." He fluffed my ears. "I still love you," he said.

I wagged my tail and licked his face to tell him I loved him, too.

Being a dog is the best thing in the world.

TWITCH
(school-yard squirrel)

That was a close call I had with that dog, and then with all those people running around School, banging doors open and yelling, "What's going on here?" and squirting each other.

As much as I know humans love squirrels, I ran out of School as fast as I could because those people were having way too much fun playing, and I knew from watching kids play that this meant *somebody* was eventually going to come and yell at them for it.

And sure enough, after all the other humans had left in their cars with the spinning lights, the man who lives next door to School brought the dog out, and he had a tight hold of his collar and was saying, "Bad dog."

Humans can be smart about certain things.

The next morning I went from window to window at School to check up on all my new friends. They were back in their cages, but otherwise they looked fine.

The humans, however, did not look fine.

The man who cleans School stood in the hallway and looked at the floor smeared with paint and water and soggy pictures. He said, "This is too much. This hurts my head. I need to lie down."

The man who lives next door to School said, "You can't do that. The visiting artist will be here any minute. The mayor will be here. The people from the newspaper will be here. You need to clean this up right now."

The children said, "Our art projects are ruined! We'll never win the contest! There's no time to start over!"

The teachers were all saying:

"Don't blame my hamster."

"Don't blame my rat."

"Don't blame my snake."

Everyone was unhappy.

"Blame the dog!" I shouted from where I sat outside the window.

But nobody paid attention because just then the person called Visiting Artist came in. He walked slowly, watching where he put his feet. He looked at the splattered, pattered-upon floor with all our paw prints, and rat-tail tracks, and slithery snake s's, and the marks made by the wheels of the cart with the fish tank, and a few bits of feather left by the macaw, and piles of glitter that had come unglued from the pictures that were floating in the puddles that hadn't dried from last night. He said, "Oh my!"

"We're so sorry about the mess," the man who lives next door to School said. "Perhaps you can come back another day?"

"Mess?" Visiting Artist cried. "Nonsense! It's perfect! Anyone can decorate pieces of paper—and walls are so obvious. It takes Vision to think to make art out of a floor! Your students are brilliant! You are brilliant! Your teachers are brilliant! You *must* all come to visit me in my studio!"

So then everyone was happy again.

And—I have to point out—that's thanks to me.

I took a little bow, sitting there on the window ledge, although I don't think the humans saw me. The turtle saw me. She waved. I think. She moves so slowly, it's hard to be sure.

It can't be easy to be a turtle. It can't be easy to be a human. I'm glad I'm a squirrel. A squirrel who is brilliant and who has Vision. Not that I'm exactly sure what *Vision* is, but I think it has something to do with being able to outrun a dog. And to make friends wherever I go.

Being a squirrel is the best thing in the world.